IT HAPPENED IN SHUSHAN

A PURIM STORY

WRITTEN BY
HARRIET K. FEDER

·

ILLUSTRATED BY
ROSALYN SCHANZER

KAR-BEN COPIES, INC.   ROCKVILLE, MD

For Benjamin
— H.K.F.

For Steve
— R.S.

Library of Congress Cataloging-in-Publication Data

Feder, Harriet K.
  It happened in Shushan.

  Summary: A fanciful version of the Purim story presented in rebus form.
  1. Purim—Juvenile literature. (1. Purim. 2. Rebuses) I. Schanzer, Rosalyn, ill.
II. Title.
BM695.P8F44   1988   296.4′36   88-2676
ISBN 0-930494-75-X

Published by KAR-BEN COPIES, INC., Rockville, MD
Printed in the United States of America
Revised 1991.

This is a story that you can help read.
Do you have to know how?
Of course not!
Do you have to be in school?
Of course not!
Do you have to like pictures?
Of course!

nce upon a time, long long ago, in a little town called shan, in the country of Persia, there ruled a foolish king  named Ahasuerus. He lived in a large palace .

Do you think he liked ruling his people?

Of course not!

Do you think he liked helping the poor?

Of course not!

Do you think he liked giving parties?

Of course!

he liked parties more than anything in the world. But the  didn't live in the in shan alone. Oh no! His wife, Queen Vashti,  lived there, too. was very, very beautiful. She was also very, very tired.

Do you think she was tired from washing ?

Of course not!

Do you think she was tired from sitting

on her throne?

Of course not!

Do you think she was tired from the parties?

Of course!

t every party, the made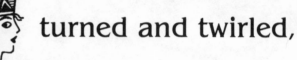

dance. Again and again,  turned and twirled,

but the  was never satisfied. He always

wanted more.

One day, the  called  to him. What

do you think he said?

Did he say, "  , I'm hungry. Get my dinner!"?

Of course not!

Did he say, "  , you look hungry.

I'll get your dinner."?

Of course not!

Did he say, "  , you must dance

at my party tonight."?

Of course!

"Can't we go to a movie?"  asked.

But the said,

"Of course not!"

(They didn't have movies in shan.)

"How about watching TV ?" asked.

But the said,

"Of course not!"

(They didn't have in shan, either.)

"If I don't come to the party will you send me away?"  asked. And the  said,

"Of course!"

nd he did. He sent away from

shan forever.

"I'll find a new queen," the  said, "one

even more beautiful than . I'll have a

contest to find the most beautiful girl

in shan."

Do you think the  of 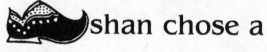shan chose a

girl named Mary?

Of course not!

Do you think the  of 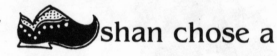shan chose a

girl named Sue?

Of course not!

Do you think the  of shan chose a

Jewish girl named Esther  ?

Of course!

 lived with her cousin Mordecai  .

Do you think  wanted to marry the  ?

Of course not!

Do you think  wanted to be queen of

shan?

Of course not!

Do you think  wanted to do her own thing?

Of course!

(She wanted to be a doctor.)

But who could say no to a ?

Soon the wedding rang out in shan.  and the  were married, and she went to live in the . Sometimes her cousin  came to visit her.

One day, met Haman   . was a very important man in the .  was in charge of all the soldiers  of the .

"When you see me,"  said to  , "you

must always bow."

Do you think you would bow to ?

Of course not!

Do you think  would bow to ?

Of course not!

Do you think  told  how he felt?

Of course!

"I am a Jew,"  told  . "I do not bow

to people, only to God." When heard

this, he became very angry. He decided to kill

all the Jews.

 put some numbers in his hat. They were

magic numbers called *lots* or *Purim.* He pulled

one out. It was number **13** . "On the 13th

day of Adar," told the  , "you must

kill all the Jews."

hen  heard this, he was very upset.

Do you think that  was silent?

Of course not!

Do you think that  would let the Jews die?

Of course not!

Do you think that  told ?

Of course!

And  went to the .

"I will give you a surprise,"  said to the .

"Can you guess what it will be?"

"Will it be a new ?" asked the .

But  said, *"Of course not!"*

"Will it be a new ?" asked the .

But  said, *"Of course not!"*

t will be something you love more

than anything else in the world."

"Will it be a party?" he shouted.

"*Of course!*" said .

"It will be the finest party you have ever seen.

Everyone in the palace will be invited, and you

must be sure to bring , too."

"I will, I will," said the , jumping for joy.

"I can hardly wait." could hardly wait also. She could hardly wait to tell the what was on her mind.

That night at the party, pointed her finger at , and told the how wicked was. "If you let that wicked

 kill the Jews," said , "he will have

to kill me, too. I am a Jew. The Jews are my

people."

hen he heard this, the  became

angry at . "I will punish this very

day," said the . And so he did.

t was such a happy day for the Jews

of shan. They declared a holiday. They

sang and danced for joy. They ate little cakes

called hamantaschen which were shaped

like the hat wicked wore.

"Let us celebrate this holiday every year,"

someone said. "But what shall we call it?" asked

another. They thought and they thought.

Do you think they called it Chanukah?

Of course not!

Do you think they called it Passover?

Of course not!

Do you think they called it Purim?

Of course!

AND WE DO, TOO!